SantaSaurus

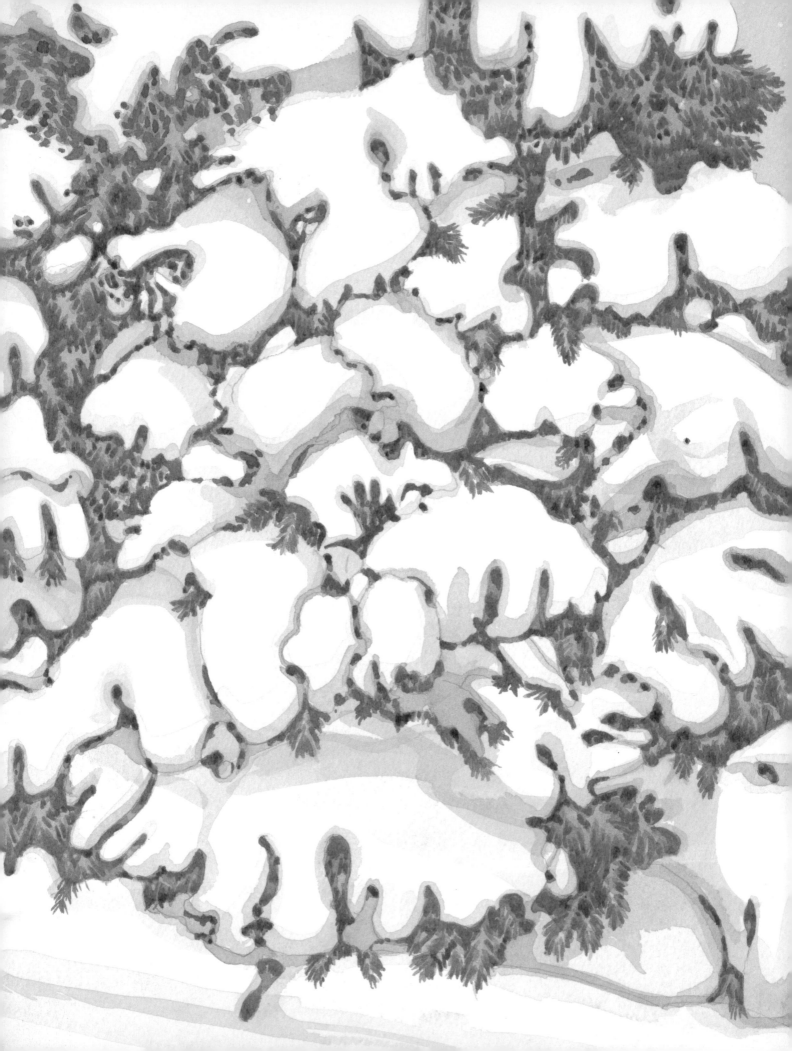

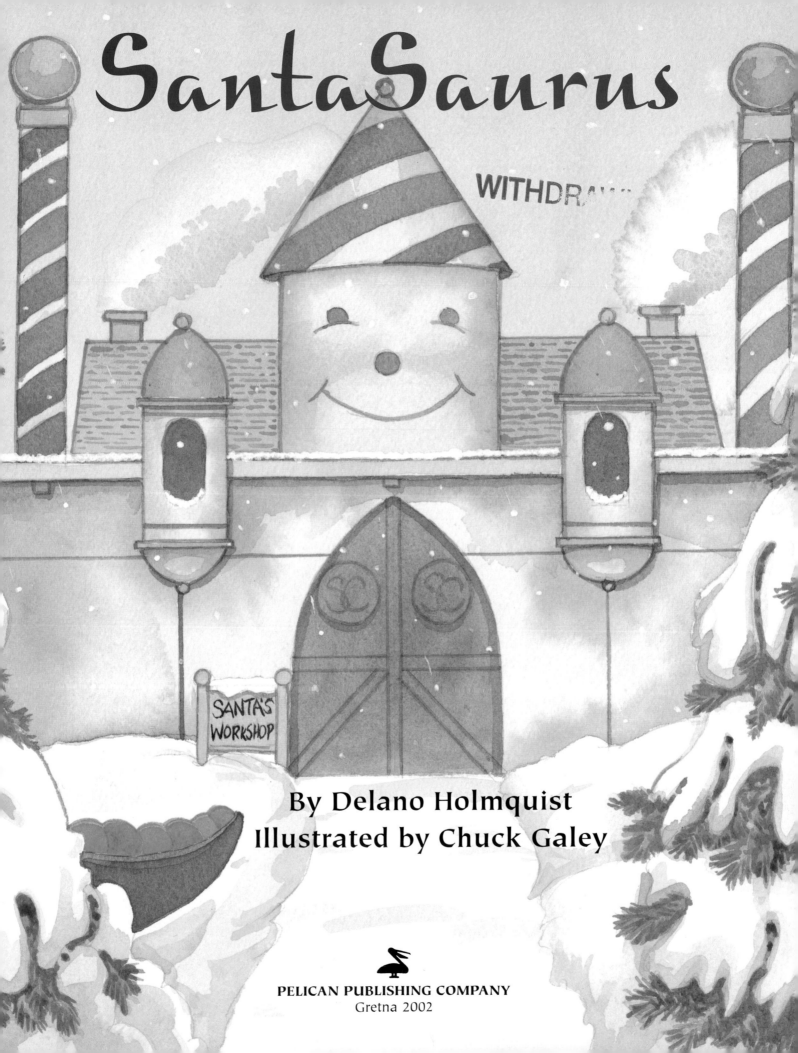

SantaSaurus

By Delano Holmquist
Illustrated by Chuck Galey

PELICAN PUBLISHING COMPANY
Gretna 2002

Thank you to those who have kept my spirit raised:
God; Dan, Jane, and Ruth Holmquist; Bob Norby; John Roth;
Nina Kupper; Nina Kooij; Gail Murray; Ann Hermes; Sherry Wiley;
Duane Olzenak; Beth Fetty; and Samantha—D.H.

To Audrey—C.G.

Library of Congress Cataloging-in-Publication Data

Holmquist, Delano.
  SantaSaurus / by Delano Holmquist ; illustrated by Chuck Galey.
      p. cm.
Summary: SantaSaurus, the Christmas dinosaur, restores Santa's holiday
Spirit with a list of good deeds that children have done throughout the
year.
  ISBN 1-56554-933-3 (hardcover : alk. paper)
  [1. Dinosaurs—Fiction. 2. Santa Claus—Fiction. 3. Christmas—Fiction.
4. Kindness—Fiction.] I. Galey, Chuck, ill. II. Title.
  PZ7.H73833 San 2002
  [E]—dc21

                    2002005666

Printed in Korea

Published by Pelican Publishing Company, Inc.
1000 Burmaster Street, Gretna, Louisiana 70053

SANTASAURUS

Once upon a time at the North Pole . . .

Padendorf and Christmas Mouse were helping pack sacks of toys onto Santa's sleigh. Everyone noticed Santa was acting strange. His nose wasn't rosy red and he wasn't laughing *Ho! Ho! Ho!* "What happened to Santa's Holiday Spirit?" asked Padendorf.

"Santa's Holiday Spirit is low," explained Christmas Mouse. "Many children wrote letters, but most only asked for toys and didn't report the good deeds they've done. It's good deeds that make the Holiday Spirit strong."

Three elves played and threw snowballs back and forth. One of the snowballs was sailing towards a nest full of baby turtledoves. Padendorf jumped high in the air, just in time to block the snowball from hitting them.

Suddenly there was a glistening swirl of snow. There stood SantaSaurus, the jolliest dinosaur you've ever seen. "You did a very kind thing, Padendorf. I'm writing it on a list of good deeds I'm sharing with Santa later today."

"Maybe that will make the Holiday Spirit grow and bring back Santa's *Ho! Ho! Ho!*" said Padendorf.

"I hope so," said Christmas Mouse.

SantaSaurus flew all over the North Pole looking for more good deeds to write on his list.

At Santa's workshop he saw Erica washing her workbench. Then he saw Andy delivering flowers to a holiday troll. At the school SantaSaurus saw elf children sharing their toys. "This is wonderful," cried SantaSaurus, as he flew to visit the reindeer.

Donner and Blitzen were painting the old barn. "When Santa sees our beautiful barn," said Blitzen, "surely that will help make the Holiday Spirit grow and bring back Santa's *Ho! Ho! Ho!*"

"I'm sure it will," said SantaSaurus.

It was getting late, and SantaSaurus had collected a
full list of all the good deeds at the North Pole that day.
He flew straight to Santa's house to share it with him.

When SantaSaurus arrived, he hopped through the kitchen, stopped to eat some Christmas cookies Mrs. Claus had just baked, then dashed into Santa's office. "Santa! I have a list of good deeds to share with you!" SantaSaurus unrolled his list. It was longer than the string of a high-flying kite. As Santa read the list, his nose grew a tiny bit rosier and his cap became a tiny bit bouncier. But he did not laugh *Ho! Ho! Ho!*

"Our elves and friends at the North
Pole do many kind things," said Santa. "I wish
I knew when children out in the world do kind things!"
SantaSaurus roared a great dinosaur laugh and said,
"Children do many kind things. Everyone knows that!"

Santa opened a drawer full of letters, picked one out, and read aloud: "Santa, Hi, It's Jimmy. Bring me a red dump-truck. My sister Jill wants a wooden easel with lots of paints! Thanks! Jimmy & Jill Larson."

"If only I knew these children shared their toys or rescued kittens or helped their grandparents. Good deeds by children make the Holiday Spirit strong. The Holiday Spirit makes Christmas possible! It makes reindeer fly. It makes me laugh *Ho! Ho! Ho!* Even miracles can happen when the Holiday Spirit is present," declared Santa. "The Holiday Spirit is a little low this year, SantaSaurus. I'm not sure what to do."

That night after eating his dinner of crunchy pinecones, SantaSaurus went to bed. He dreamed about Santa and the children of the world. He suddenly awoke with a brilliant idea!

He would go and visit Jimmy and Jill Larson and make a list of all the good deeds they did in the past year. Those good deeds would make the Holiday Spirit grow and bring back Santa's *Ho! Ho! Ho!*

He flew to Santa's house and tiptoed into the office, silent as could be. There he found the letter from Jimmy and Jill Larson that Santa had read to him. According to the address, Jimmy and Jill lived in a town called Alexandria.

SantaSaurus hurried to the reindeer barn. Blitzen helped him study the world map. SantaSaurus was soon flying to Alexandria.

The next morning in Alexandria, a man opened his door to get the newspaper, but when he saw SantaSaurus, he slammed the door in fright. Dogs barked and people honked their car horns as SantaSaurus walked down the street.

SantaSaurus stopped to ask children playing in a park where Jimmy and Jill Larson lived. They took SantaSaurus's hand and skipped alongside him as they wound their way around the park and through the city to Jimmy and Jill's house.

Jimmy and Jill were very surprised to see SantaSaurus at their door. SantaSaurus explained to everyone that the Holiday Spirit was low and he needed a list of their good deeds to bring back Santa's *Ho! Ho! Ho!*

"Last week Jimmy helped me pick up my toys, and he made a card for our neighbor. He also taught a little boy how to play marbles!" said Jill.

"And Jill gave her allowance to help a hungry child," said Jimmy, "and she always tells the truth."

"Very kind!" exclaimed SantaSaurus, writing his list. Soon all the children were telling him the good deeds they'd done, like cleaning their rooms, helping elderly neighbors, listening to their parents, and much more. Soon the list was long as a river, long as a rainbow!

SantaSaurus was having such a wonderful time that he forgot it was Christmas Eve! He needed to get back to share the list with Santa. He thanked the children, wiggled his tail, and flew back to the North Pole.

SantaSaurus arrived just as Santa and Mrs. Claus were finishing dinner. He handed the list over to Santa. As Santa read, SantaSaurus was so excited he hopped from one foot to the other, wondering what Santa would say.

"Look at all the good deeds they've done! The children of Alexandria are very kind indeed," said Santa. At that moment Santa's nose grew a gazillion times rosier and his cap was the bounciest it had been in years!

And best of all, he laughed *Ho! Ho! Ho!* over and over. That Christmas was the merriest ever, because everybody, including Santa, remembered how good children are and how much love is in their hearts.

And that is how SantaSaurus became the official keeper of Santa's Good Deed List.